Al

Written by Jo Windsor
Illustrated by Richard Hoit

Rigby

Marion loved to clean.
She cleaned the windows.

"All clean, all clean!"
said the parrot
in his cage.

All clean, all clean!

3

She cleaned the walls.
She went up
and down with the
vacuum cleaner.

"All clean, all clean!"
said the parrot
in his cage.

All clean, all clean

5

She cleaned the floor. She went around and around with the vacuum cleaner.

"All clean, all clean!" said the parrot in his cage.

All clean, all clean!

7

Then . . .

Marion cleaned
the parrot's cage.
Up and down,
and up and down . . .

9

Wh-ooo-sh!

The parrot went
into the vacuum cleaner.

"Look out! Look out!"
shouted the parrot.

Look out! Look out!

11

"Oh dear! Oh dear!"
said Marion.
She took the parrot out
of the vacuum cleaner.

"Dirty parrot, dirty parrot!"
said the parrot.

Dirty parrot, dirty parrot!

13

Marion cleaned the parrot.

"Thank you, thank you," said the parrot.
"All clean! All clean!"

14

A Flow Diagram

Guide Notes

Title: All Clean
Stage: Early (2) – Yellow

Genre: Fiction
Approach: Guided Reading
Processes: Thinking Critically, Exploring Language, Processing Information
Written and Visual Focus: Panel, Flow diagram

THINKING CRITICALLY
(sample questions)
- What do you think this story could be about?
- What do you know about parrots?
- How can you tell Marion liked to clean?
- Look at pages 10-11. Why do you think the parrot went up the vacuum cleaner?
- How do you think the parrot would feel in the vacuum cleaner?
- Look at pages 12-13. How do you think Marion feels?
- Look at page 13. Discuss "parrot" talk. Can parrots really talk?

EXPLORING LANGUAGE

Terminology
Title, cover, illustrations, author, illustrator

Vocabulary
Interest words: parrot, dirty, vacuum cleaner
High-frequency words (reinforced): to, she, the, all, said, from, his, went, out, you
New words: clean, around, took, thank, loved, then, oh
Positional words: into, up, down

Print Conventions
Capital letter for sentence beginnings and name (**M**arion), periods, exclamation marks, quotation marks, commas, ellipses